To my son and best friend,
I cannot even begin to describe how
proud of you I am. You have created a
whole world and filled it with lovable
characters. Within that, is a beautiful
message about family and community
that I believe we could all learn from.
Never stop being you.

All my love, Dad.

A Tale of 10 Dragons

Dragons

Book 1

Chapter 1

A long time ago there were nine white dragons, they each lived in their own cave around the mystical island Thunder. There was also a bad purple dragon who lived in a volcano, he eats the horses on the island. Every day the good dragons try to stop him but the bad dragon always catches one. The good dragons eat grass with the horses and play in the field.

Chapter 2

One day the horses and dragons were playing together; they got so hot that they had to stop at the pond for a drink. When they arrived, they spotted the purple dragon waiting for them. "Hand over those horses" the purple dragon said.

"Why don't you eat grass with us" said Stump, the smallest white dragon.

"But you could join us and live in the empty cave" said Lumpy, the lumpiest white dragon.

"Leave me alone" the purple dragon shouted before flying away empty handed. This went on for years, nothing ever changed.

Chapter 3

Over time the purple dragon was seen less and less, until eventually he disappeared completely. One day the white dragons called a meeting to make a plan to find the purple dragon.

"I will search the sky because I have the biggest wings" said Stomp in a booming voice.

"We will search the meadow" Blossom and Daisy said softly together.

"I can fly too y'know" said Breezey, "I will fly around our caves."

Chunk the chunkiest dragon turned his chunky head and said "me and Spike will search around the volcano".

Spike shook his spiky tail and nodded his head.

"I have no idea" said No-idea, the dumbest dragon.

"You just stay here and stay out of our way" growled Stomp. When the meeting was over the dragons set off on their search.

Chapter 4

Blossom and Daisy walked through the sunny meadow, searching all the flowers for the purple dragon. When there was nowhere left to check the two dragons returned to the stone table. Breezey flew low around the island, swooping up and down between the caves. When he found nothing but rocks, he reported back to the others at the stone table. Lumpy, Stump and No-idea waited with the horses at the meeting spot; they noticed Blossom Daisy and Breezey walking towards them. The dragons shared what they had found, they decided to find the others who had not come back. As Stomp flew high above the island, he saw no sign of Old Purple anywhere. But he did see all of his friends marching towards the volcano, he decided to fly on ahead. When he arrived, he spotted Chunk and Spike waving from the doorway of the volcano.

"Come quick" Chunk shouted, "we found him!"

13

Chapter 5

The dragons gathered inside the large cavern of the gigantic volcano, staring down at the hot lava below. At the bottom of the pit was a huge purple dragon with a big fat belly, covered in lava from his tummy to the tip of his tail. Fortunately, dragons are fireproof, but lava is sticky and Old Purple was stuck. "What are you doing down there?" Stomp asked, as the others began exploring the cave. "What do you mean, what am I doing?" Old Purple replied, "this is my home. What are you doing?" Daisy looked down at the purple dragon and said "we were worried about you, grumpy pants!"

"We looked all over the island for you" Blossom called from somewhere in the cave, "what happened?" The purple dragon turned his head towards Blossom and sighed, "the volcano is erupting and I am too old to escape". "Too fat more like" said Stump from deep inside the cave, "perhaps" groaned Old Purple. "Whatever the cause, I'm trapped and I'm not getting out" he said sadly. The dragons stopped snooping through the cave and gathered around the purple dragon, feeling very sorry for him. For the first time ever, the ten dragons sat together and listened to each other's stories.

17

Chapter 6

After hours of storytelling the volcano began to tremble and the dragons started to panic.

"Oh no" they all yelled,

"what do we do?" Daisy cried.

"I have no idea" said No-idea,

"why didn't you call for help?" Stomp asked.

"I did call, over and over again, but my volcano is too far from your caves" Old Purple replied.

"If only you had been our friend, you would have been safe in the caves with us" Blossom said with tears in her eyes.

"If you ate grass instead of horses you could have flown to safety" Breezey added. The volcano shook so hard that all the rocks inside began to crumble and fall.

"Time to go" said Old Purple,

"What about you?" Lumpy asked.

"No time to argue it's now or never" the purple dragon said, the volcano spat hot lava and the dragons ran to safety as quickly as dragons can. When they arrived safely back at the meeting spot Stomp checked on each of the dragons, luckily none were hurt. But Stomp only counted eight dragons. He could see Lumpy, Stump, Blossom, Daisy, Chunk, Spike, Breezey and himself.

"Where is No-idea?" He asked,

"I'm here" said a voice from behind the bushes.

As the voice appeared the dragons gasped. "What is that you are holding" asked Stomp.

"I have no idea" said No-idea, walking towards the stone table.

"Where did you find it?" Stomp asked, more firmly this time.

"I have no idea" said No-idea, walking faster now.

"So why did you take it then?" Stomp demanded.

"I have no idea" said No-idea, now running towards the others. All of a sudden, his foot slipped on a tree root and the large round purple mystery object went flying through the air, until it landed with a hard THUD in the middle of the table. The dragons froze, but the purple thing began to wobble. It shook more and more until...

CRACK!

The thing broke in half and the dragons stared in amazement. Out crawled a tiny purple dragon.

"Where am I?" It asked.

"You are home" said Stomp and the dragons greeted their new friend.

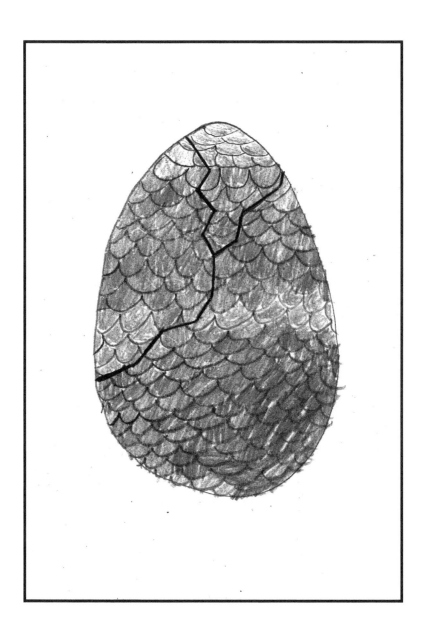

Young Purple's Journey

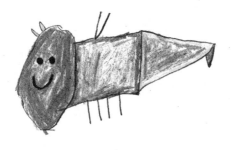

Book 2

Chapter 1

One day on the mystical island Thunder, the dragons were playing together in the meadow. It had been five years since Young Purple had hatched from the egg that No-idea found. He was growing bigger every day. Young Purple had enjoyed living with the white dragons, he loved his cave by the sea and all his horse friends. As the dragons played with the horses, Young Purple couldn't help but notice how different he looked to all his brothers and sisters. For starters: he had purple scales, his spike was orange, he didn't like the taste of grass and he had two small green horns. There were other differences too; all of his brothers and sisters knew their parents, but Young Purple did not. In the past when he had asked about them, the others always said that they would tell him when he was older. He was now five years old and he felt grown up enough, so he decided it was time to find some answers.

29

Chapter 2

The next day, Young Purple left his cave at sunrise. He was too excited to sleep. He knew the others wouldn't be up yet so he decided to go for a walk. He left his cave and walked while daydreaming until he arrived at the meeting spot. Stomp waited at the big stone table, it seemed like he had been there a while.

"Where might you be going?" Stomp asked cheerfully, before taking a big bite of some grass. Young Purple didn't expect to find anyone awake and the sound of Stomp's deep voice startled him. He couldn't think of any good excuses so he decided to tell the truth.

"I want to know where I came from," Young Purple said with a squeaky voice, feeling a little less confident than the day before. He cleared his throat and continued. "I am old enough to know the truth and if you won't tell me then I will find out by myself!"

Stomp chuckled and swallowed the grass he was chewing.

"I have been expecting this chat for a while, so ask away."

Young Purple's mind was racing with hundreds of questions, he thought for a moment, but the words came out by themselves.

"Where are my parents?"

"I never knew your mother but your father and I became friends towards the end."

"What was he like?"

"Well, he was lonely and he was a bit of a grumpy dragon."

"Why was he lonely, didn't he play with the horses?"

"No little dragon he didn't play with them, he ate them."

"HE ATE THE HORSES, YUK!"

"Indeed."

"Where did he live?"

"Not a nice place, it was hard and empty except for your dad."

"What happened to him?"

"There was a terrible accident and he didn't make it out."

Young Purple felt dizzy from all the new information, so he continued on his walk, hoping to clear his head.

Chapter 3

Later that day, Young Purple arrived at the pond. The sun was shining brightly in the sky, it was a hot day. He took a big drink from the pond but he was still hot and sweaty, so he tucked his wings in and dived head first into the cold water. When he opened his eyes, he saw a family of five fish, they were playing so nicely they didn't notice the purple dragon. He tried to say hello but only bubbles came out. The fish were startled by the dragon and swam away as fast as they could. Alone in the water, Young Purple thought about his dad and felt a little sad. He paddled to the edge and climbed out, he shook the water off and noticed two faces staring at him.

"Hello little dragon" said Blossom.

"Hi girls" Young Purple replied.

"What were you doing down there?" Daisy asked.

"I was just going for a swim to cool down, what were you two doing?"

"We were also trying to keep cool in the shade of this

willow tree," Blossom said.

"You seem a little down today, what's up?" Daisy asked. Young Purple told them about his conversation with Stomp, as well as his plan to learn more about his dad. When the young dragon had finished talking, both of the girls were close to tears.

"How sad, that all you know about your dad are his troubles" Blossom sobbed.

"That's why I need to find out more, I know my dad was more than just a grumpy dragon!" replied Young Purple. After a long silence,

Daisy said "I think you should speak to No-idea".

"Why should I speak to No-idea?" Young Purple asked.

"Because, he is the one who found your egg." Blossom answered.

Shocked and amazed, Young Purple went off in search of No-idea. He felt re-energized by the new information.

39

Chapter 4

After several hours, Young Purple spotted two dragons along the coast by the caves. As he approached, he began to identify the two dragons; they both had wings but only one seemed to be able to fly. It was Breezey and No-idea. Young Purple watched as Breezey swooped and looped through the air, while No-idea looked more confused than ever. The young dragon sat, hypnotised by the awesome display. When Breezey's feet were safely back on the ground, Young

Purple made his way over to say hello. The two dragons greeted him warmly, with wings flapping and tails wagging.

"What were you doing?" Young Purple asked, impressed by what he had seen.

"I have no idea" said No-idea.

"Are you kidding me!" Breezey snapped. "All day I have been trying to teach you how to fly, were you even watching?"

"Yes, I was watching but I still have no idea how it is done."

Breezey rolled his eyes and

took a deep breath. Before Young Purple had a chance to speak, Breezey shot up into the air and spread his wings.

"I will show you once more, pay attention" he called down. Breezey landed gently on Lumpy's cave. "First, you need a high place" he said. "Next, you need a nice big jump". Breezey leaped off of the cave, while the others watched closely. He fell through the air, gaining more and more speed. "Finally, spread your wings" and Breezey did. He swooped up sharply, using his large wings to catch the air. He glided smoothly over the dragons and landed safely on the ground. The two dragons turned to face Breezey, who looked straight at No-idea and said "Your turn". No-idea slowly climbed to the top of Lumpy's cave, using his sharp claws to grip the rocks. When he reached the top, a very sleepy and lumpy dragon appeared.

"You woke me up" Lumpy said with an enormous yawn.

"Sorry, I'm learning to fly and I need a high place to start from" No-idea replied.

"In that case, show me what

you have learnt."

No-idea jumped high into the air, just as he'd been shown. He folded his wings and dived down toward the sea. At the last moment he spread his wings...

SPLAT!

He hit the water hard. After a lot of splashing, he reached the shore. Breezey wasn't impressed. "Pathetic!" He snarled. "Try again, from the top".

45

Chapter 5

After many hours, the sun began to set and the clouds began to darken. Tired and hungry, Young Purple and No-idea made their way to the meeting spot for dinner. Waiting for them was Stump, Spike, Chunk, Blossom and Daisy. On the stone table was a delicious feast made up of apples, lemons, oranges, nuts, berries, leaves and lots of grass. Without a word, No-idea sat down and began to fill his mouth with as much food as he could. After all his training he was as hungry as Chunk. Young Purple took his place at the table between Stump and No-idea, unlike the others, he did not have an appetite. Instead of eating, he thought about the final question he wanted answered. As the dragons ate and talked amongst themselves Young Purple waited patiently. Finally, he couldn't wait any longer. "Where did I come from?" At that moment there was a blinding flash of light and the deep rumble of thunder. Everybody fell silent, all eyes were on the little purple dragon. The lightning continued in the distance, striking the tip of the volcano repeatedly as it always did during a storm. This mystical event is where the island gets its' name. After a short silence, No-idea mumbled "I have no idea". Stump didn't look up from his food. Without thinking, he said "of course you do! That was the day we all went to the volcano". The dragons immediately froze, their eyes wide open. *The volcano!* Young Purple couldn't believe he hadn't thought of it before.

"Why didn't you tell me this sooner?" He demanded.

"The volcano is not a safe place" warned Chunk. The others muttered in agreement, including Spike, who wagged his tail and nodded his head.

"That's not good enough!" Snapped the little dragon. "I had a right to know" he continued in a calmer voice.

"We are sorry, we thought we were keeping you safe" said Blossom.

"It doesn't matter now. I need to see this for myself" Young purple replied. Without another word, the little dragon ran off through the bushes before anyone could stop him. The others started to panic. They were worried about the little dragon in the colossal storm, No-idea most of all. Without thinking, he chased after Young Purple. He couldn't see the little dragon, but he knew exactly where he was heading. He began to run in the direction of the volcano. His feet moved faster and faster until they left the ground. He spread his wings and flew.

51

Chapter 6

No-idea soared high above the trees, gazing down at the world below. Everything seemed so small and unimportant from up high. He couldn't believe his eyes, He wondered if he was dreaming. No, he was almost certain he was not asleep back in his cave. He was still unsure how he had done it, but at that moment he had bigger things to worry about. He had to find his small purple friend. The volcano loomed in the distance, with the storm clouds thickening overhead. He dipped his head, straightened his tail and flapped his wings as hard as he could.

Elsewhere, Young Purple ran through the bushes and the trees. His head was swimming and his heart was racing. He knew the other dragons cared about him and he loved them too, but he was furious with them for keeping his history a secret. He knew they only did what they thought was right in order to keep him safe, but his anger burned as hot as dragon-fire. He used this anger to fuel his legs, running faster than he ever had before. Eventually the trees cleared and the soft green grass gave way to cold hard stone. The volcano towered high into the clouds above, it truly was the biggest thing he had ever seen. With no entrance in sight, the little dragon walked around the foot of the thunderous mountain. The lightning continued to strike the peak every couple of minutes. When the latest bolt struck, Young Purple noticed a beam of light escape from the side of the volcano. He moved closer to get a better look, when he came upon a large doorway. With a deep breath, he gulped and stepped inside. The inside of the cavern was as dark as night, lit only by the moon and the occasional flash of lightning.

High above the trees No-idea strained against the fierce winds, working hard to remain in the sky. Eventually he arrived at the peak of the volcano. He circled the vast crater, scanning the cavern for signs of life. This was difficult because the only real light came from the lightning, but he continued to look.

Inside the volcano, Young

Purple stood face to face with his dad. In the dim moonlight, the massive dragon appeared to be sleeping. However, in the flashes of lightning the truth was clear. Old Purple had turned to stone. The young dragon couldn't keep his feelings in any more, he let out a single cry before tears filled his eyes.

"Why did you leave me?"

Young Purple screamed over and over again, until he could scream no more. There was another flash of lightning, followed by a shout.

"Hello down there!"

"No-idea?"

"That's me."

"You're flying! How did you manage that?"

"I have no id..."

ZAP!

A bolt of lightning hit No-idea right between the eyes. He fell from the sky, down to the cavern below. He crashed straight into the statue of the old dragon.

"Oh, you stupid clumsy dragon! You destroyed it. That was all I had left of my dad and now it's gone forever."

Young Purple was heartbroken, he was about to

turn and run when there was a deep booming cough from within the pile of rubble.

"Not quite."

The old dragon stepped into the moon light. He began to say something else, but then he collapsed.

"Dad?!"

59

Legend of the Golden Dragon

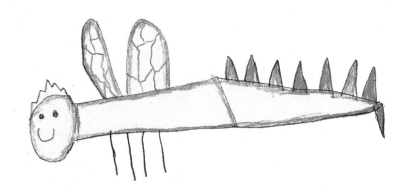

Book 3

Chapter 1

On the mystical island Thunder, all of the dragons gathered around the stone table. They could not believe their eyes. Stretched out before them was a very familiar looking, old purple dragon.

"What in the world is he doing here?" Stomp asked, gazing down at Young Purple.

"We found him inside the volcano" the young dragon replied.

"Then we helped to carry him back here" added Chunk.

Spike slammed his tail against a tree in agreement.

"What's wrong with him?" Blossom asked.

"Will he be okay?" Daisy added.

At that moment, the old dragon woke up.

"Where am I?" Old Purple croaked. Young Purple shuffled his way to the front of the group. Being the smallest, he wanted to make sure he would be seen and heard. "Don't worry dad, you're safe." The old dragon shifted his weight so he could look down at Young Purple, "dad?" he repeated. The two dragons stared at each other; nobody made a sound. After a few minutes, Stomp broke the silence. "It has been five years since we last saw you, a lot has changed. Even you don't look like the old fat dragon we left behind."

"Five years in stone has taken its toll on me" Old Purple said, before coughing severely. When he caught his breath, he turned again to his son. "I'm afraid I have statue sickness my boy. I'm sorry we couldn't meet under better circumstances, but I am really glad to see you. You look just like me". Young Purple stood stunned; the news of his father's illness was most shocking. Lumpy was next to speak,

"I don't understand. What's statue sickness?" Surprisingly, it was Stomp who answered.

"It is an ancient dragon disease that troubled our ancestors, from a time when we all lived in volcanoes. Usually, it would only affect a foot or a tail. The dragon would then lose the limb and regenerate a new one. But I have never heard of a dragon's entire body being overrun before, there may be no way to fix him." Chunk asked the question that was on everybody's mind, "what's going to happen to him?"

"He is turning to stone from the inside out" Stomp replied.

"That's horrible!" Daisy cried.

"There must be a cure?" Blossom asked. Old Purple coughed and cleared his throat. "Maybe once, but I'm afraid she hasn't been seen in over eight hundred years."

Young Purple sensed a small glimmer of hope. "What do you mean, she?" The young dragon asked.

"She is the oldest of our kind, the Legendary Golden Dragon."

Chapter 2

The next morning, all of the dragons were buzzing with excitement. Everybody was talking about the Legendary Golden Dragon. They had gathered at the stone table at sunrise, armed with a million questions. However, Stomp had expected as much. He was waiting for them when they arrived.

"Where do you think you are going?" Stomp asked the group. Stump stepped forward, "we have questions for old grumpy pants" he said.

Stomp spoke in a deep voice. "Need I remind you that Old Purple is very sick, he needs his rest." The dragons returned to their caves, feeling a little guilty. Stomp glanced around to make sure he was alone; he was happy to see that the others had listened to him. He pushed his way past the bushes, to find Old Purple exactly where they had left him the night before.

"How are you feeling today?" Stomp asked. Old Purple opened one eye to look at Stomp and simply replied "worse". Stomp seated himself in front of the stone table, he wanted to speak without anyone overhearing.

"In that case, we need a plan and quickly." Old Purple didn't say a word, but now he had both eyes open. Stomp continued.

"Look, the others will keep coming with more and more questions. I say we give them some answers and maybe, even find you a cure."

"I admire your bravery Stomp, but as I already told you, that dragon is long gone. Even if she was still around, she only visited this island once."

Stomp thought about this for a moment, then an idea began to form in his mind. He smiled at Old Purple and asked "Where was she last seen?"

The old dragon looked puzzled, so he answered with another question.

"Why, what are you thinking?" Stomp and Old Purple talked until sunset, going over every detail of Stomp's plan. By the time the others arrived for dinner, they had it all worked out. Stomp decided to let them eat before revealing his plan; they would need their strength for what was to come. Once dinner was out of the way, Stomp slammed his tail against the ground to get everybody's attention.

"We have a plan, now I need you all to listen" ordered Stomp. He gave everybody a job to do. Blossom and Daisy would stay and care for Old Purple, Chunk and Spike's job was to stay and gather food and Lumpy would look after the horses. The rest of the dragons made sacks for supplies by weaving leaves together tightly. Next, they filled them with food and water, then said their goodbyes to the rest of the gang. They met on the beach and shared out the sacks of supplies. Stump still had questions.

"How exactly is this supposed to work Stomp?"

"I will carry you on my back, Breezey will take Young Purple and No-idea only has himself to worry about. He is still learning, after all." Young Purple spoke next.

"You still haven't told us where we are going."

"North" Stomp replied.

"Over the ocean?" Breezey asked, a little worried.

"That is the only way to reach

the mystical island Ice" Stomp replied. No-idea was more confused than usual, he asked "Why there?"

"We are going to find a cure" Stomp said with a smile. Young Purple was so shocked he couldn't speak. Stomp continued.

"We are going to find the Legendary Golden Dragon!" Stomp slung Stump across his back and took to the air, the others soon followed.

77

Chapter 3

The dragons had been at sea for many weeks, they all felt exhausted. The food and water they had packed was running dangerously low and there was no land in sight.

"I don't know how much longer I can keep this up" Breezey wheezed.

"I know what you mean, I'm shattered" said Stump. Stomp rolled his eyes and let out a low growl from deep in his chest, he was growing tired of Stump's annoying jokes. At that moment, Young Purple stood up.

"I think I see something" he said. As the dragons flew closer, the fog cleared to reveal a small island made of rock.

"Let's stop and rest" said Stomp. The dragons landed on the large rock and immediately dropped their sacks. Stomp, Breezey and No-idea fell to the floor, then started to snore.

"I guess they really needed to rest" said Young Purple.

"I just hope it doesn't take another month for them to recover" Stump replied.

After a few hours the smaller

dragons began to grow restless. Young Purple decided to stretch his legs and take a look around the rock. Unfortunately, there wasn't much to look at. The rock was mostly black, except for patches of green seaweed that had washed up from the waves. For an island, it was rather small. Young Purple doubted it would have been big enough to hold everybody if the others had come along. After a few laps of the rock, he realised he could walk around the entire edge in just a few minutes. On his tenth lap, he noticed something new. Along the water's edge, there was a large round white spot. It seemed to be softer than the rock, perhaps a jellyfish had got stuck.

"Hey Stump, check this out" he called. Stump joined Young Purple and began to inspect the spot. The dragons argued over what they thought it was.

"It's clearly a jellyfish"

"Don't be a fool, obviously it's a mushroom"

Their voices grew so loud, the others woke up with a growl and a grumble.

"What is all that noise about?"

Stomp groaned.

"I found something strange, we can't decide what it is" Young Purple replied. Stomp, Breezey and No-idea stretched their wings before joining the others. They each examined the white spot, but no one knew what it was. No-idea began to speak but Stomp cut him off.

"Don't say it, we are all clueless" he said. At that moment, the rocks around the white spot closed shut. When they opened again, there was now a smaller black spot in the centre of the white one. Stomp sat bolt upright.

"We need to go. Now!" Stomp shouted. The dragons knew better than to argue with their leader. Stump jumped on to Stomp's back, while Breezey Scooped up Young Purple. The water around the rock began to bubble and the ground started to tremble. The dragons launched into the air. From up high, it looked like the rock was sinking.

"What about the sacks?" Breezey asked.

"No time. Start flying" ordered Stomp. The dragons flapped their wings as hard as they could, hoping to get far away from the rock. All of a sudden, the sea below them erupted. Where the rock used to be was now a tall black pillar of rock and razor-sharp teeth. The huge jaws snapped shut inches away from No-idea's tail. The sea monster fell back to the water below, creating a giant tidal wave. The wave rose high above the dragons before crashing down on them. Everything went dark.

When the dragons awoke, they found themselves scattered along a beach made entirely of ice.

85

Chapter 4

Back on the mystical island Thunder, the rest of the dragons were hard at work. They had all accepted their new jobs without complaint, each dragon took pride in their work. Everyday started with a delicious breakfast, Spike and Chunk only picked the freshest fruit and nuts. After breakfast, Lumpy would take the leftover food down to the horses. When all the horses have eaten, it's time to groom them. After a good brushing, Lumpy would spend the afternoon playing with the horses in the meadow. Meanwhile, Spike and Chunk spent their day searching the island for tasty ingredients to use for dinner. They had to search a different spot each day to avoid stripping the bushes bare. It was Blossom and Daisy however, who had the toughest job. As well as caring for Old Purple, they found themselves looking after all the remaining dragons. Their day started at sunrise, they washed their faces and sharpened their claws before waking the others. No matter what, they always liked to look their best. Before they ate their own breakfast, they fed Old Purple. He didn't always like what they brought him, but after five years in stone, he never wasted a single crumb. The girls spent the rest of their day speaking with Old Purple. Occasionally, the boys would come to them with a problem. Without Stomp around, it was down to them to find a solution. They always did. With all their new responsibilities, Blossom and Daisy had aged four years in just a month. In that time, they had each grown a beautiful pair of wings. Unlike the boys, who's wings were blue, Blossom's wings were a soft pink colour, whereas Daisy's were bright yellow. They could not fly as well as Breezey or Stomp, but they were both making progress. Old Purple had been surprisingly helpful, he had been flying longer than any of the other dragons. One afternoon, Old Purple was teaching the girls about different air currents. He had just finished explaining how the weather affected the air, when he became very dizzy. He tried to call for help, but his head felt heavy and his sight turned dark. When he came to, Blossom and Daisy were standing over him.

"You passed out again didn't you?" Blossom asked, concerned.

"I'm fine" he replied sternly.

"No, you're not, it's getting worse" Daisy added. It was true. Old Purple felt weaker every day, his appetite was shrinking and his cough was getting worse. He would not admit it though, he was much too proud to show any sign of weakness. Some of the changes could not be hidden so easily, more than half of his body was now cold and grey. That night after dinner, Old Purple overheard the others talking.

"He won't last much longer" said Chunk.

"We have to stay hopeful" Lumpy replied.

"I hope the others return soon" said Daisy.

So do I Old Purple thought to himself, before closing his eyes to sleep.

Chapter 5

Stomp and the rest of the search party had been scouring the mystical island Ice for two weeks without success. In that time, they found many wonderful things but no sign of the Legendary Golden Dragon. The plants and animals that lived on the island were very different from the ones back home. There were no horses in sight. Instead, packs of wolves roamed the island. The trees were not green, but pink with cherry blossom. Even the water was different, it was colder and fresher than anything the dragons had tasted before. After splitting up in the morning to cover more ground, the dragons regrouped to share information and eat some lunch. They discovered the meeting spot on their first day on the island, complete with its' own table made of ice. The dragons were all seated at the table, sharing portions of carrots and potatoes. Food was not so easy to find, unlike back home.

"This is hopeless" groaned Young Purple, in between

mouthfuls.

"The kid is right; it appears as though we may be the only dragons on this island" said Stump. The gang grew silent, each of them considering the possibility. Breezey broke the silence.

"Come on guys, we have to be optimistic."

"That would be easier to do with a hot meal in our bellies" replied Stump.

"I am afraid that without the heat of our volcano, cold carrots and potatoes is as good as it gets" Stomp reminded them.

"I have an idea" said No-idea, to everyone's surprise. The dragons all looked at No-idea, waiting for him to explain. He continued.

"Well, our last two adventures both ended at our volcano. This island has a volcano and it's one of the few places we haven't searched yet. I bet that's where we'll find her." The gang was speechless. Stomp considered the idea for a moment.

"Good idea, Let's go guys" he commanded. They left immediately, taking the rest of their lunch with them. They trekked over the snowy meadow, past the frozen pond and through the icy fields. After several hours, they eventually arrived at the ice volcano. At first glance, it appeared to be an enormous iceberg. Upon closer inspection, the dragons noticed that the ice was just a shell surrounding the stone beneath. The dragons searched the outskirts of the volcano, hoping to discover a way inside. When none could be found, they decided to fly up to the peak. The air atop the volcano was much colder and

the wind was blowing fiercely.
"Hey No-idea, take young purple. I'm going in for a closer look" Breezey shouted over the noisy winds. Young Purple leaped from Breezey's back and landed on No-idea safely. Breezey swooped down and began to circle the crater. All of a sudden, the wind fell still and the temperature plummeted. Out of the volcano shot a cloud of pure white snow, narrowly missing Breezey's nose.

"Be careful!" Stomp called down. Breezey descended into the volcano, landing softly on the cavern floor.

"You had better come down guys, you're going to want to see this" he called up to the others. The dragons carefully joined Breezey and their hearts sank. Standing before them was the Legendary Golden Dragon, frozen in ice. Young Purple knew they would never be able to dig her out in time to save his dad, he began to sob. The others hung their heads low in defeat, all except Stomp. Their fearless leader could not believe that after all they had endured, they were going to fail now. He felt a deep rage burning in his chest. Facing the golden dragon, he opened his jaw to let out an angry roar. Instead, white hot flames shot from his mouth, reducing the ice to a steamy puddle. The dragons stared in amazement as the steam cleared and the Legendary Golden Dragon emerged.

101

Chapter 6

The Legendary Golden Dragon addressed the search party, smiling a big toothy smile.

"Thank you all for rescuing me, I thought I would remain trapped forever." The dragons were too shocked to speak, so she continued.

"Usually, a little ice wouldn't bother me. However, this blasted volcano kept freezing me over and over again. If there is anything that I can do for you, name it and it's yours." Young Purple snapped out of his daze, he walked over and stood before the gold dragon. She was the most beautiful thing he had ever seen, each scale shined like the sun.

"Please, save my dad" the little dragon pleaded. The Legendary Golden Dragon looked down at Young Purple, smiling once again.

"If I can, I will little one. What's wrong with him?"

"He has statue sickness; we need one of your scales to fix him."

"It would be my pleasure, where is he now?"

"The mystical island Thunder, our home."

"Then there's not a moment to lose, we must leave at once." The dragons groaned at the thought of another long journey. The Legendary Golden Dragon sensed their unease.

"Friends, worry not. I can take the two small ones; we'll be home in no time" she said reassuringly.

"With respect, it took us a whole month to get here" said Stomp. The gold dragon chuckled to herself.

"Stay above and behind me as

we fly. The heat from my scales will aid your speed and keep you aloft without effort" she replied. The dragons prepared to leave, filled with renewed hope. As soon as they were ready, they flew out of the volcano and headed towards the sunset and the sunset and the home that awaited them.

Meanwhile elsewhere, Old Purple was in big trouble. All but his head had turned to stone and he was beginning to lose hope. Blossom and Daisy had remained at his side for the past week, never leaving him. They had grown fond of their old teacher in recent weeks, they couldn't bear the thought of him being alone. That evening, the dragons all dined with Old Purple, even the horses joined in. They knew the old statue was no longer a threat to them. As the dragons ate, Old Purple told tales of his many adventures and the magical places he had seen. That night, none of the dragons made it back to their caves. Instead, they all curled up to sleep around Old Purple. The following morning, the dragons awoke to an alarming cry.

"Argh! My eyes, I can't see!"

The dragons rubbed their eyes, then looked with horror at Old Purple. The statue sickness had spread to his face, all but his mouth was now covered in stone. The others tried to reassure him but his stony ears could hear no more. Just as it seemed that all hope was lost, Daisy spotted something bright on the horizon.

"Guys, look!" At first, it looked as if a second sun was rising. As the golden light approached, they could see the shape of a dragon within.

"They did it!" Chunk cried. The returning dragons were flying faster than anyone thought possible. The search party landed on the beach and ran straight to the big stone table, where the others awaited them. The Legendary Golden Dragon knelt before Old Purple. Next, she carefully removed a scale from her tail. Then she gently placed it under his tongue. As his mouth closed, the stone spread and covered the last piece of him. The dragons froze.

"It didn't work" said Blossom.

"Wait, look" Stomp replied.

The statue began to crack and from the cracks shone a bright golden light. More and more appeared until at last, the stone fell away. Standing before them was Old Purple, alive and well. However, he was not the same dragon he once was. His green horns and tail spikes were now orange and his blue wings were now a web of orange and gold. In fact, every single purple scale had been turned to gold.

"Dad, you look magnificent!" Young Purple exclaimed. The others muttered in agreement and spike slammed his tail in approval. Old Purple looked at his new scales with pride.

"Thank you all so much, especially you" he said to the Legendary Golden Dragon.

"It was an honour. If not for your family, I would have been trapped forever" she replied. *My family* Old Purple thought to himself as he smiled. The dragons celebrated with a mighty feast that lasted an entire week. Everybody was invited, the horses too. They played lots of games and told many stories; the Legendary Golden Dragon told the best ones. Tales of magic and monsters, distant lands and peculiar creatures called man. When the feast was finally over, the gold dragons made a surprising announcement.

"It is time for us to leave" Old Purple said. The gang fell silent, so he continued to explain.

"We are going to find a home for old dragons to live in peace."

"But you can't leave, I need you" Young Purple yelled.

"No, you don't, you already have the perfect family right here" he replied kindly. Young

Purple realised his dad was right. All of his previous anger had melted away. After all their adventures together, he had no more doubts. He knew now that family had nothing to do with appearances.

"Fear not little one, he will not be alone" added the Legendary Golden Dragon. Young Purple smiled; he was glad that the gold dragons had each other. One by one the dragons said their goodbyes, wishing their gold friends good luck on their next adventure. At sunset, the gold dragons were ready to leave. They said one final farewell and took to the sky. The others watched from the beach, thinking back on their time together.

"So, what have we all learned from this?" Stomp asked the group.

"I have no idea" said No-idea. Everybody burst out laughing. As they laughed together as a family, the gold dragons vanished into the distance and the sun slowly set.

The End

About the Author

Jacob started writing A Tale of 10 Dragons during the 2020 global lock down, when he was six years old. What started as a handwriting exercise for homework, evolved in to a full-time adventure for both father and son. As the months passed by, Jacob's cursive improved but so did his enthusiasm and stamina. He decided he wanted to continue writing books, making them even bigger and better than before. He is now 7 and the proud author of a trilogy, which we hope you enjoyed.

Lightning Source UK Ltd.
Milton Keynes UK
UKHW050340140121
376908UK00007B/160

9 781034 205494